P9-EFI-822

To P & G, Zia, and the Zapp-Dealey cousins, with love and olives.
Many thanks to Amy Lennex and awesome agent Deborah Warren.
— Erin

Especially for Archie
— Nick

Text Copyright © 2013 Erin Dealey
Illustration Copyright © 2013 Nick Ward

All rights reserved. No part of this book may be reproduced in any manner
without the express written consent of the publisher, except in the case of brief
excerpts in critical reviews and articles. All inquiries should be addressed to:

Sleeping Bear Press™

315 East Eisenhower Parkway, Suite 200
Ann Arbor, MI 48108
www.sleepingbearpress.com

© Sleeping Bear Press

Printed and bound in the United States

10 9 8 7 6 5 4 3 2 1

Library of Congress Cataloging-in-Publication Data

Dealey, Erin.
Deck the walls : a wacky Christmas carol / by Erin Dealey ;
illustrated by Nick Ward.
pages cm
Summary: Provides new, food-themed lyrics to the classic Christmas song
as a family gathers for a meal that involves building a snowman from
tomatoes, playing olive hockey, and being bored by aunts and uncles.
ISBN 978-1-58536-857-0
1. Christmas music--Texts. 2. Children's songs--Texts. 3. Humorous
songs--Texts. [1. Christmas music. 2. Humorous songs. 3. Songs.]
I. Ward, Nick, 1955- illustrator. II. Title.
PZ8.3.D3415Dec 2013
782.42'1723--dc23
[E]
2013002581

Deck the Walls!

A Wacky Christmas Carol

Erin Dealey * Illustrated by Nick Ward

PUBLISHED BY SLEEPING BEAR PRESS

Deck the walls with mashed potatoes!

Fa la la la la   la la la la

Make a snowman with tomatoes.

Feed the dog our peas and carrots.

Fa la la la la la la la la!

Food tastes better when you wear it.

Fa la la la la la la la la

Sneak a cookie. Grams made dozens.

Fa la la la la   la la la la

Olive hockey with the cousins.

Fa la la la la   la la la la

Shot on goal! The gravy splashes!

Fa la la la la la la la la!

Catch the dish before it crashes.

Fa la la la la la la la la

Uncle Harvey stands before us.

Fa la la la la   la la la la

Why do aunts and uncles bore us . . .

Fa la la la la   la la la la

. . . with their talk of how we're taller?

Fa la la   la la la   la la la!

Maybe they're just getting smaller!

Fa la la   la la la   la la la

Fast away the cousins scatter . . .
Fa la la la la   la la la la

while the grown-ups clear the platters.

Fa la la la la   la la la la

Dash outside to frosty weather.

Fa la la la la   la la la la!

Thankful we are all together!

Fa la la la la   la la la la

Christmas Sugar Cookies

Ingredients

1 pound soft butter or margarine
2 ½ cups sugar
2 teaspoons vanilla
4 eggs
5 ½ cups flour
2 teaspoons baking powder

In a large bowl cream butter, sugar, and vanilla using a mixer. Add eggs one at a time, beating for one minute on high speed after each addition. Mix flour and baking powder together in a separate bowl. Gradually add flour mixture to butter and sugar mixture. Chill the dough for several hours or overnight.

When ready to bake, preheat oven to 350° Fahrenheit. Remove dough to a floured surface. Using a rolling pin, roll thin and cut with cookie cutters. Bake for 8 to 10 minutes. Remove from cookie sheet and allow to cool. Frost and decorate as desired.

Recipe courtesy of Mrs. Donna Lennex

Deck the Halls

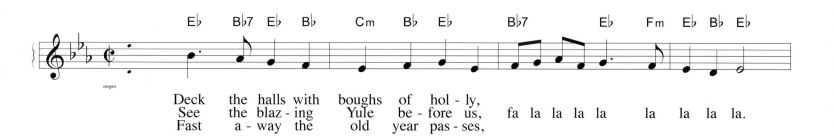

Deck   the halls with   boughs of hol - ly,
See   the blaz - ing   Yule be - fore us,   fa la la la la   la la la la.
Fast   a - way the   old   year pas - ses,

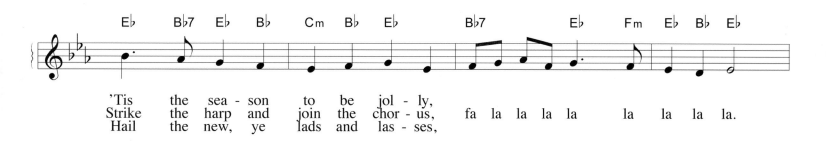

'Tis   the sea - son   to be   jol - ly,
Strike   the harp and   join the   chor - us,   fa la la la la   la la la la.
Hail   the new, ye   lads and las - ses,

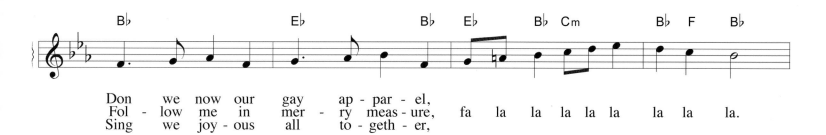

Don   we now our   gay   ap - par - el,
Fol - low me in   mer - ry meas - ure,   fa la la la la la la la la.
Sing   we joy - ous   all   to - geth - er,

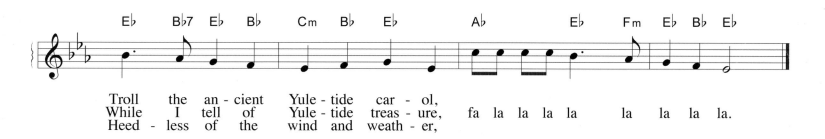

Troll   the an - cient   Yule - tide car - ol,
While   I   tell of   Yule - tide treas - ure,   fa la la la la la la la la.
Heed - less of the   wind and weath - er,

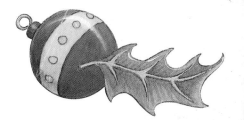